# PRAISE FOR
# DAEDALUS LEO

Robert Williscroft has done it again. The idea of jumping from orbit using little more than a spacesuit and a re-entry pack goes back at least to Heinlein's *Starship Troopers*, and I've used it myself, but Williscroft puts a new twist on it as "Tiger" Baily makes the jump in *Daedalus LEO*. A great tale, with his usual attention to detail.

**– Alastair Mayer**
**Author of *The T-Space Series***

*Daedalus LEO* by Robert G. Williscroft is even more exciting than *Daedalus*, the first story in this series. There are more thrills, more near-escapes, more humor, and more spectacular sightseeing of the Earth far below. More romance too, for that matter. This time around the author has upped the ante. It's the first manned LEO (Low Earth Orbit) drop, and instead of 80 klicks, the *Gryphon 10* has to drop 160, or twice as far. And of course, despite the best efforts of Derek "Tiger" Baily and his team, almost everything seems to go wrong.

Those who are the first to enter a new frontier incur a great risk. Numbers are not enough. Planning is not enough. Safeguards are not enough. As Derek says, "until we actually made the first drop, all we had were numbers that we hoped made sense." You have to constantly be prepared for the unexpected, for times "when all hell breaks loose!" This is a great adventure, even better than the first, and I'm glad I was along for the ride.

**– Professor John B. Rosenman, Norfolk State University**
**Former Chairman of the Board, Horror Writers Association**
**Author of *The Inspector of the Cross Series***

*Daedalus LEO* is about the unimaginable, yet somehow, Robert Williscroft not only imagined it but made it real—and breathtakingly thrilling.

The idea of a human being deliberately placing himself in low earth orbit to carry out a proof of concept mission is an image as fresh, and yet disturbing, as they come. Mind you, Derek "Tiger" Baily is an extraordinary human, and this is no ordinary story. Those of us growing up in the space age know full well that reentry from orbit is terrifyingly dangerous. The fires of reentry consume foolish mortals who make the slightest mistake. And mistakes and problems arise aplenty in Tiger's trial run.

At risk is the future of American special warfare operations. Will Baily's risky adventure be the birth of something entirely new, or yet another failed blue-sky concept ending in cinders?

– **Dr. John R. Clarke**
**Author of *The Jason Parker Series***

Author Robert Williscroft delivers the goods once again with *Daedalus LEO*, a short sci-fi story that chronicles Lt. Commander Derek "Tiger" Baily's flight from low-Earth orbit in a wingsuit. To call the Gryphon-10 a wingsuit is a stretch, but I think it conveys the idea without introducing spoilers. As with all of Williscroft's work, the writing is tight and realistic. The characters are three-dimensional against a backdrop of excitement, thrills, and cliff-hangers. And the science in this sci-fi is damn accurate. In fact, much of the plot and details are science fact, and part of the fun, as with the work of the late great Michael Crichton, is trying to discern the thin line between truth and fiction. *The Starchild Trilogy* and *Daedalus* short stories are highly recommended to sci-fi/thriller aficionados. Five stars!

– **Dr. Dave Edlund**
***USA Today* Bestselling Author –**
***The Peter Savage Thrillers***

# DAEDALUS LEO

## SWIC Drop from Low Earth Orbit

# DAEDALUS LEO

## SWIC Drop from Low Earth Orbit

## Robert G. Williscroft

Fresh Ink Group
Guntersville

*DAEDALUS LEO*
**SWIC Drop from Low Earth Orbit**

Copyright © 2019
by Robert G. Williscroft
All rights reserved

Fresh Ink Group
An Imprint of:
The Fresh Ink Group, LLC
Box 931
Guntersville, AL 35976
*info@FreshInkGroup.com*
*FreshInkGroup.com*

Edition 1.0      2019

Cover art by Anik / FIG
Illustration by Anik / FIG
Book design by Amit Dey / FIG
Covers by Stephen Geez / FIG

Cataloging-in-Publication Recommendations:
F1CO28020 FICTION / Science Fiction / Hard Science Fiction
FIC002000 FICTION / Action & Adventure
F1CO2801 0 FICTION / Science Fiction / Action & Adventure

Library of Congress Control Number: 2019911112

ISBN-13: 978-1-947867-59-8  Papercover
ISBN-13: 978-1-947867-60-4  Hardcover
ISBN-13: 978-1-947867-61-1  Ebooks

# DEDICATION

*This story is dedicated to the U.S. Navy SEALS
who may someday make this story a reality.*

# TABLE OF CONTENTS

# ACKNOWLEDGEMENTS

*Several people contributed to the creation of this book.*

*Most significantly, my wonderful wife, Jill, whom I first met when I returned from a year at the South Pole conducting atmospheric research, and who finally consented to marry me nearly thirty years later, pored over this story with her discerning engineer's eye. She kept my timeline honest and made sure that regular readers could understand fully the arcane details of the Launch Loop and the Gryphon.*

*Hard science fiction authors Alastair Mayer, John Clark, and Prof John Rosenman, and USA Today bestselling author Dave Edlund reviewed the manuscript and offered their editorial insights.*

*Lauren Smith from Fresh Ink Group applied her professional associate publisher's eye to improve the story.*

*It goes without saying that any remaining omissions, errors, and mistakes fall directly on my shoulders.*

**Robert G. Williscroft, PhD**
**Centennial, Colorado**
**September 2019**

# FOREWORD

*Slingshot* is my novel about constructing the world's first Space Launch Loop. The book was launched August, 2015, at the International Space Elevator Conference in Seattle, and resides on the desk of every Space Elevator scientist in the world. Space Launch Loops appear in the subsequent books in *The Starchild Trilogy*, and anyone familiar with my *Trilogy* knows all about these commercial space launch systems.

When I discovered the *Gryphon* rigid wingsuit, the *SWIC Daedalus Files* pushed themselves into my consciousness. The first story is a consequence of Slingshot's skyports effectively being eighty km tall wingsuit *base-jumping* towers. This second story follows naturally from the first.

SEAL derring-do is real, the science and technology are real, the *Gryphon* rigid wingsuit is real, and I suspect that something like SWIC will become part of the U.S. Navy SEALS in the relatively near future.

Robert G. Williscroft
Centennial, Colorado
September 2019

# CAST OF CHARACTERS

## SEALS Winged Insertion Command (SWIC)

**Capt. Brad Nelson**—Commanding Officer SWIC.

**Lt.Cdr. Tom Spitzer**—Executive Officer SWIC.

**Mother**—Controlling computer in each *Gryphon-10*

**Max**—Full-size *Gryphon-10* simulator

## SEALS Winged Insertion Command Three (SWIC-3)

**Lt.Cdr. Derek "Tiger" Baily**—Narrator, Commanding Officer SWIC-3.

**Lt. Jim Fox**—Executive Officer SWIC-3.

**Master Chief Jerry Boldt**—Master Chief SWIC-3.

**Senior Chief Bob Baxter**—Master Chief Boldt's second.

## Launch Loop International (LLI)

**Sam Davidson**—Slingshot Director.

**Apryl Searson**—Chief Diver EMT.

## Houston Flight Control

**Disembodied voice**—Houston Flight Control Director.

# DAEDALUS LEO

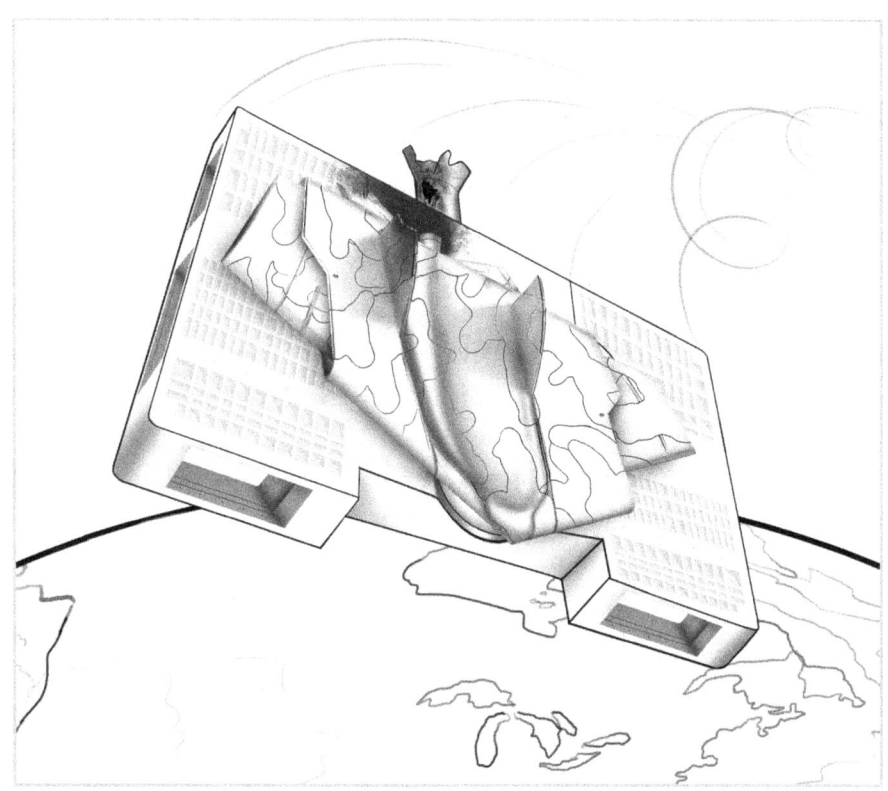

## LOW EARTH ORBIT

"**W**hat the fuck!" I yelped as the rear of my *Gryphon-10* pallet tilted sharply upward while the nose yawed to the right. Then the whole thing started to tumble in a spiral fashion as the kick thruster continued its burn. Mother wasn't stopping it, so I activated the manual jettison override. I watched the burning kick thruster spiral ahead of me and then flare out. I lost it in the glare of the morning sun.

"I got a problem here, Control," I said as calmly as I could manage. I described what had happened from my limited perspective. "Mother, deploy the tethered holocam and make a full external inspection," I ordered as I began to get my act together.

"Tiger, we are calculating your modified orbital parameters right now," Master Chief Boldt told me with his calming voice. "Okay…here it is. You are nominally still at one-hundred-sixty klicks, but your orbit has shifted right by twenty-two-point-five-degrees. That passes over central Mexico, well south of Baja. You're stable, but you have to get control of your tumble so we can calculate a new set of drop parameters."

"Roger," I said.

"Tethered holocam deployed," Mother said softly.

Mother controlled the bird-size tethered holocam to ensure that it maintained a stable position relative to my corkscrew. Using additional short gas bursts, I maneuvered the holocam down the length of the pallet and *Gryphon-10* looking for damage.

"Jesus H…," I muttered as it moved to my stern. "Are you getting this, Control?"

"Roger, we are."

The back end of the pallet was partially melted, and a large chunk was missing from my right fin.

"Mother, can I survive reentry with that fin damage?"

"Negative, Tiger," Mother said softly, "Probability of complete structure failure one hundred percent."

## CORONADO—SAN DIEGO—SEVERAL DAYS EARLIER

Derek "Tiger" Baily—you may remember me. The *Gryphon-7*? My 80,000-meter base jump from the Fred Noonan Skyport on *Slingshot*? Well…so much for fifteen minutes of fame, but you still can see *Gryphon-7* at the Smithsonian, and you can read about my exploit if you dig a little bit.

I'm still with the Teams—the U.S. Navy SEALS, but now I command SEALS Winged Insertion Command Three, SWIC-3 for short. I suspect somebody in the hierarchy goofed after I completed that 80,000-meter base jump, but I got orders to OCS—that's Officer Candidate School for you non-military types—and ended up back at SWIC-3 as a freshly minted Butter Bar—Ensign. We continued our *Gryphon* development with me as XO under Lt.Cdr. Tom Spitzer. Senior Chief Jerry Boldt was still with us, in line for Master Chief. By the time my old CO Brad Nelson made Captain, they gave him command of SWIC, assigned Tom as his XO, and I got command of SWIC-3 along with early promotion to Lt.Cdr. Like I said, somebody really goofed up there, but who am I to argue with them? Besides, they sent me Lt. Jim Fox as XO. He had come up through the SEAL ranks like me, and I couldn't have gotten a better man to back me up.

My assignment, SWIC-3's assignment, was probably impossible to accomplish. I figured that just made it interesting. All Capt. Nelson wanted was for SWIC-3 to do a *Gryphon* drop from LEO—Low Earth Orbit.

## CORONADO—GRYPHON-10

*Gryphon-7* had been relegated to the annals of SEAL history. *Gryphon-8* incorporated the structural changes resulting from my water landing, causing the craft to act more like a surfboard when upside down in the water, and giving it external propulsion—basically incorporating a water-jet. *Gryphon-9* changed a lot of things. It had larger wings with more fuel capacity, more powerful jet with throttle control, longer tail, and more intuitive control interface.

*Gryphon-10* is the baby we would use for the LEO drop. It had some radical changes including full body armor with circulating fuel for heat protection, an increased surface area using dimples, wrinkles, and rolls that dramatically boosted heat shedding, and it incorporated a new type of polymer that was stronger, lighter, and more heat resistant than anything before. The biggest change, however, was the guidance computer unit—we called it Mother—that was designed to act on its calculations before the human pilot was even aware of them. *Gryphon-10* was still man-transportable, although more ungainly than the old *Gryphon-7* model. Its unpowered glide ratio was 14-1, and it could fly 100 level klicks under power.

Unlike *Gryphon-7* that started at eighty klicks with zero velocity, *Gryphon-10* would start at 160 klicks moving at orbital velocity. To survive the jump, *Gryphon-10* had to shed as much velocity as possible as quickly as possible. We needed to get from Mach 26 down to about Mach 3. What we'd do was to dip down into the atmosphere shedding speed until drag brought the temperature to the limit, and then skip back out of the atmosphere to let the suit cool off. Then back in again, shed more speed, heat to the limit, and back out to cool off. And again…and again…using a bit of fuel for each dip until we slowed to about Mach 3. Then dip for the last time, and stretch out the glide for max distance—and land at the desired destination. We ran the problem in reverse, letting the computers work out the number and details of the skips in order to specify where in our equatorial orbit we would need to commence the drop. We threw every variable we could think of at the problem and calculated the drop for 10,000 different scenarios.

## CORONADO—MAX

To help plan the drop, we constructed Max—a full-scale simulator that cost a good deal more than the actual *Gryphon-10*. Everyone in SWIC-3 ran Max dozens of times. I did the first run and crashed and burned big time. With practice, we got the system down and a feel for what to do during each skip into the atmosphere.

Now, here's the rub. Everything we did up to this point was theoretical—even with Max. We gave Max every scrap of reentry information we could find, everything we knew about upper atmosphere weather, every bit of physics that could possibly bear on the problem. Mother knew everything Max knew and was connected to worldwide live feeds. In a real drop, Mother would know everything possible about the path ahead, and everything Max had done in similar situations during simulation runs. Mother would have every possible edge to give us the desired outcome. Yet…until we actually made the first drop, all we had were numbers that we hoped made sense.

## SLINGSHOT—EQUATORIAL PACIFIC

Beyond Max, we ran real jumps using the full *Gryphon-10* from Fred Noonan Skyport on Slingshot to Kiritimati and even to Tabuaeran Atoll about 100 klicks further north. We didn't challenge a squall like I had done on the first Kiritimati jump, but I was confident that the *Gryphon-10* could have handled it with ease. We did soft belly landings, near-shore water landings, and blue-water landings. We had no problems—none at all.

That was encouraging, to say the least.

## LEO—UNMANNED DROP

I sent Master Chief Boldt to Baker Island with four SWIC-3 members. They lifted to Amelia Earhart Skyport with the empty *Gryphon-10* attached to a cargo pallet. After ensuring that everything was fully ready for the drop, they launched the pallet with its load.

The process of obtaining a circular orbit was automatic until the actual launch of *Griffon-10*. I controlled that from our Flight Control Center (FCC) at Coronado.

✳

I initiated the drop sequence and then sat at the Command Console, watching Mother do her thing. We shed velocity with three dips, and a few minutes later, *Gryphon-10* was circling about two klicks above San Diego Bay shedding the last of her forward velocity and altitude.

Ten minutes later everyone but me pushed through the FCC door as *Gryphon-10* spiraled to a picture-perfect landing ten meters from the door.

## CORONADO—MANNED DROP PREP

Every SWIC-3 member wanted to do the first manned LEO drop—including me. They chose me to do the first static drop from Slingshot back in my enlisted days because I was easily the most experienced wingsuit man in the Teams—that's why they recruited me in the first place. But now, I was part of *they*. I still was the most experienced wing-suit man in the Teams, more so now than ever. Furthermore, I had more experience in *Gryphon-10*, both in Max and for real drops, than anyone else—close to as much as everyone else combined. Not only did I have more Max drops under my belt, but I also had more Max disasters, and I had found creative ways to extricate myself from several of them. But I also was CO of SWIC-3. Despite what you see in holobroadcasts, commanding officers do not normally do everything personally. They surround themselves with good people, and then they assign the best people to the task at hand.

I know that Capt. Nelson had several high-level discussions with his Team boss, and I suspect the discussions went even higher. What we were attempting was still classified above Top Secret, but our success would give a dramatic new insertion capability to the generals and admirals who make the big plans. I'm sure the interest went all the way to the White House.

In the end, I was ordered to the assignment, Lt. Jim Fox was given temporary command of SWIC-3, and Master Chief Jerry Boldt was temporarily assigned as Executive Officer. Senior Chief Bob Baxter took over for Master Chief Boldt, and the Team members supplied their best efforts in support.

## HOWLAND & BAKER ISLANDS—PRELAUNCH

As I departed Coronado for North Island Airfield with Senior Chief Baxter and six SWIC-3 Team members, I quipped to the rest of the Team, "This is the first leg of my roundtrip, guys. I'll see you back here in two-and-a-half days." It turned out that was not exactly how it happened, but we didn't know that then.

We had already spent three days going over every single part of *Gryphon-10* and its launch pallet, and we did the same with its twin, a fully operational backup system. Then I went over both systems again myself—just to be sure. Both systems waited for us strapped down in a big Navy supersonic transport aircraft on the North Island tarmac under a brilliant blue sky speckled with puffy cirrocumulus clouds.

The entire remaining SWIC-3 team and Capt. Nelson himself saw us off. We jetted down the runway, lifted through the sparse clouds into the stratosphere, and turned toward Hawaii as we accelerated to nearly Mach 2.

Four hours later, with one refueling stop in Hawaii, we rolled to a stop at Amelia Earhart International Airport under a blistering equatorial sun. Thousands of sooty terns, lesser frigatebirds, and masked boobies filled the sky, kept clear of aircraft by a sonic system that was inaudible to the human ear.

At the end of the tarmac near the entrance to Launch Loop International (LLI) Howland headquarters, two Chinooks waited with cargo bays open, twin rotors drooping as if wilting in the hot tropical sun. Senior Chief Baxter and his six guys remained with the aircraft to supervise the unloading of the two pallets and their loading into the much tighter Chinook interiors.

I strolled slowly through the humid air toward the headquarters building to meet with the current Slingshot director, Sam Davidson. As I turned toward the double front doors, they opened and out walked Apryl Searson.

"Tiger Baily, as I live and breathe! It's really you, isn't it?" She ran up, threw her arms around my neck, and gave me a kiss the like of which I had not received in a very long time.

"I've been here several times in the last few months," I said. "Where were you?"

"Been at the Atlantic site working with Margo on the new launch loop," she said nuzzling my neck. "What're you doing here?"

"If I told you, Apryl, I'd have to kill you," I said with a grin.

"Will you have any time for me before you leave for LEO?" she asked with a twinkle in her blue eyes.

"Schedule's pretty tight," I told her, "but a guy's gotta sleep…"

She stuck out her tongue at me. "…or not," she whispered as she disentangled herself. "When are you lifting to the skyport?"

"Later this afternoon, when we have thoroughly checked both systems out—both the Senior Chief and me."

"In these or your flightsuit?" she asked, stroking my chest.

"I'll change into my flightsuit after I talk with Sam," I told her.

❋

I spent fifteen minutes with Sam Davidson. He had been briefed on our operation and was concerned about any possible hitch in his 24/7 schedule of throwing people and cargo into space. His launch operation was tight by any definition: One personnel or cargo capsule every three minutes, each adding to LLI's bottom line. That's 480 daily launches, typically broken down into 2,000 metric tons of cargo and eighty personnel capsules. That's a lot of freight and people, and my operation would impact it negatively.

"Sam," I said as I stood to leave, "I know we're cutting into your schedule, but you're being well paid for the inconvenience." I shook his hand. "Besides, think of the glory!"

He grinned and slapped my back as I left. "Good luck, Tiger! I'm glad it's you, and not me."

❋

Apryl was waiting for me outside Sam's door, my folded flightsuit in her arms. She winked and indicated with a toss of her blond, pixie-cut hair for me to follow her. Intrigued, I did, despite my tight schedule. We entered a small conference room. Apryl locked the door behind us, threw her arms around my neck, and wrapped her legs around my waist. She planted a kiss on me that eclipsed her earlier one on the steps.

After we came up for air, things progressed rapidly, and all I can say is that it was a good thing the room was soundproofed.

I left the conference room several minutes later, somewhat the worse for wear, dressed in my flightsuit—still pretty much on schedule. Apryl promised to give my clothing to Senior Chief Baxter.

❋

By the time I got to the Chinooks, Senior Chief Baxter and his guys had both pallets loaded and were tightening straps over the fairings, cinching them to tie-downs in the chopper decks. Baxter split the guys up, and then he took one Chinook, and I took the other for the short flight to Baker Island.

The choppers landed right next to the loading rail and disgorged the pallets. An articulating boom crane loader rolled up under control of one of the socket crew who deftly hoisted the first pallet over the rail where another crew member attached it to a launch dolly directly behind the personnel capsule designated for us. Then he did the second one, that would remain at the socket, ready to lift should it be needed. Senior Chief Baxter carefully checked each component of each pallet-dolly unit, and then I did it again. Everything checked out.

Senior Chief Baxter glanced at me, and I nodded. "Board up!" he told the guys.

The five-minute trip up to Amelia Earhart Skyport was just as much of a rush as the first time.

## AMELIA EARHART SKYPORT—PRELAUNCH

At Amelia Earhart Skyport, eighty klicks above Baker Island, the capsule tilted to horizontal, sealed against the skyport lock, and the door opened inward. There was Apryl Searson tossing me a coquettish smile. Apparently, she had caught the first available capsule following our tryst. As I stepped into the reception area, Apryl brushed my lips with hers and whispered in my ear, "Before you leave, Tiger, find three minutes for me!" Senior Chief Baxter pretended not to notice, but his guys all grinned at me. One flashed me a thumbs-up.

The capsule closed behind us, the lock sealed, and a gantry crane moved the capsule out of the way.

"Okay, guys, suit up!" Baxter ordered, and a minute or so later, the pallet arrived.

With skytower traffic stopped, the guys hustled through the personnel lock. They removed the fairing and stowed it, and then they prepped the pallet with its *Gryphon-10* payload, swinging the wingsuit pod cover to vertical on its hinges like a clamshell. Baxter once more examined every part of the pallet and wingsuit. If it was humanly possible, he was not going to let something happen to the Skipper (me!) on his watch during this historic LEO drop. He took his time, oblivious to the queued-up freight pallets and passenger capsules waiting down at Baker Socket. As he finished, he signaled to me in the main skyport lounge area to suit up for *my* final system check.

"Time to go," I said to Apryl who was snuggled against me on a couch overlooking the broad, colorful band of stars that we know as the Milky Way; only out here it looked more like a multi-colored, diamond-studded bracelet spanning the sky.

The skyport crew had left us alone during the setup and systems check, and even now they gave us as much privacy as possible. Apryl nuzzled my neck and then kissed me passionately.

"Come back to me, Tiger, and tell me all about your fantastic adventure!"

Little did she or I know what lay in store.

※

After disentangling myself from Apryl, I suited up. Our suits were an advanced version of the old NASA flightsuits incorporating high-pressure oxygen bottles and electronic carbon-dioxide scrubbers. A pair of TBH (Thomas, Bird, and Hellbaum) hypergolic jet boots that slipped over the suit feet and calves completed the getup. The boot fuel valves were controlled by a microswitch under each big toe.

I stepped through the personnel lock onto the dock and commenced a detailed inspection of the pallet and wingsuit. Like Senior Chief Baxter, I took my time. It was my ass on the line, and I wanted to be sure that everything was nominal.

My team stood around chatting quietly on their private circuit, watching everything I did to ensure I missed nothing. I kept open a private circuit with the Senior Chief and went through the checklist with him, item-by-item. I was focused for about a half-hour, and as I

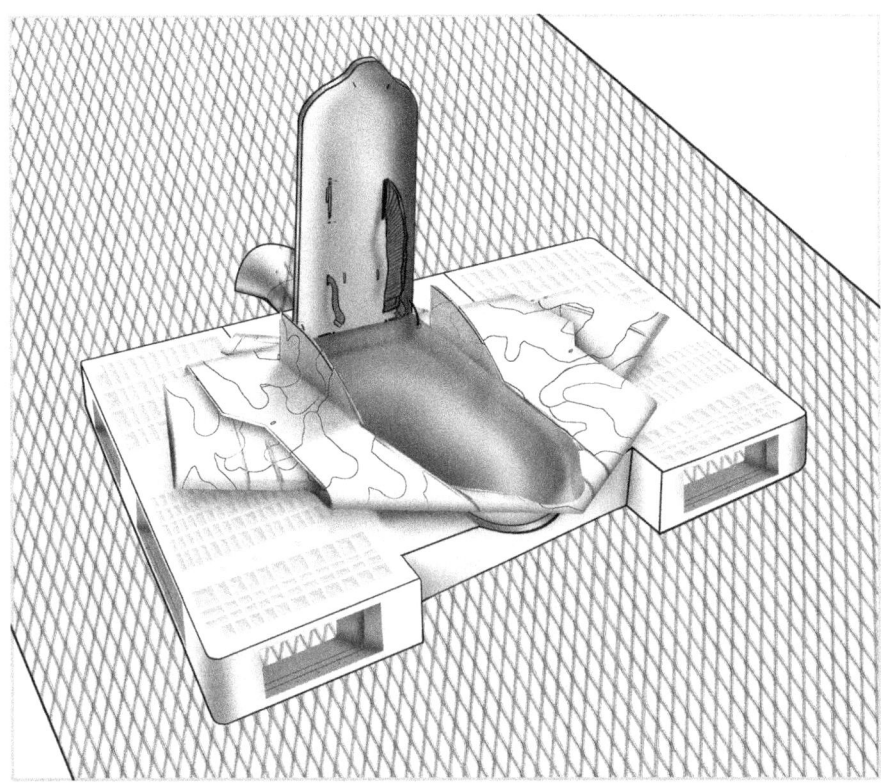

finished, I looked up at the transparent port between the dock and the skyport lounge. Apryl's face filled the port. I waved a gauntleted hand at her, and she blew a kiss back. My guys roared their approval, although I could only see this by the expressions on their faces—the dock remained silent.

I stepped onto the pallet, backed up against the pod cover, and allowed the crew to strap me in. Unlike *Gryphon-7*, where my arms were securely strapped to the wings, on the *Gryphon-10* my arms were free to move from the wings to my body within the encasing carapace. This was a lot more comfortable than the older version, but I still could not scratch my back. My legs were strapped in very much like the *Gryphon-7*, as was my body. Then the crew swung down the pod cover with me attached just like a closing clamshell. They sealed the edges all around, pressurized it, and checked for leaks.

So far, this was exactly like the several static drops I had already made from Fred Noonan Skyport in the *Gryphon-10*. As I felt the cool breeze from my air supply against my right cheek, I told the Senior Chief that I was ready for the final countdown.

## AMELIA EARHART SKYPORT—LAUNCH

"**B**ase, Bird—comm check."

"Loud and clear, Tiger." It was Master Chief Boldt. His calm voice was reassuring.

"We completed all checks and are transiting to the rail," I said. "Systems nominal up here."

"Roger that…Base systems nominal."

"Mother, state your status," Boldt ordered.

"Standing by to launch." Mother's voice did not sound artificial but rather had a soothing, contralto tone.

"We're ready when you are," Boldt said.

I felt the gantry lift the pallet and move down the track. I knew the routine, but my direct vision was limited to down and a bit side to side. I could turn my head inside the transparent helmet, but the helmet was locked into the carapace. I activated my heads-up display so I could monitor what was going on around me. The gantry moved the pallet to the kick thruster platform, and then backward to attach the kick thruster. The kick thruster is a reigniteable solid-fuel rocket. This always worried me a bit. I'm not a rocket scientist, but I know a lot about rockets. Shutting down a burning solid-fuel rocket is no simple task. LLI did this using an iris-like very strong magnetic field to slice through the solid fuel column just above the burn. They had never experienced a misfire, so the odds were in my favor, but this time *I* was riding the pallet. I wasn't safely tucked into a capsule that could withstand atmospheric reentry in case something went wrong.

The gantry moved the pallet over the rail where a launch pouch was attached. Its purpose was to couple magnetically to the rail, accelerating the pallet at three-gees until it reached LEO orbital velocity. Simple to tell, but complex in doing.

"Final systems check," I announced over the general circuit. "Bird systems nominal."

"Mother nominal." Mother's calming voice filled my helmet.

"Flight Control nominal," Master Chief Boldt said. "On my count: Five, four, three, two, one…Launch!"

## SLINGSHOT RAIL—COUPLED

One moment we—the pallet, *Gryphon-10*, and I—were hovering above the rail. The next, we surged forward, gently at first, and then rapidly built to three-gees, with me taking the gees through my body to my feet. I could still feel the Velcro straps securing my legs inside the upper carapace.

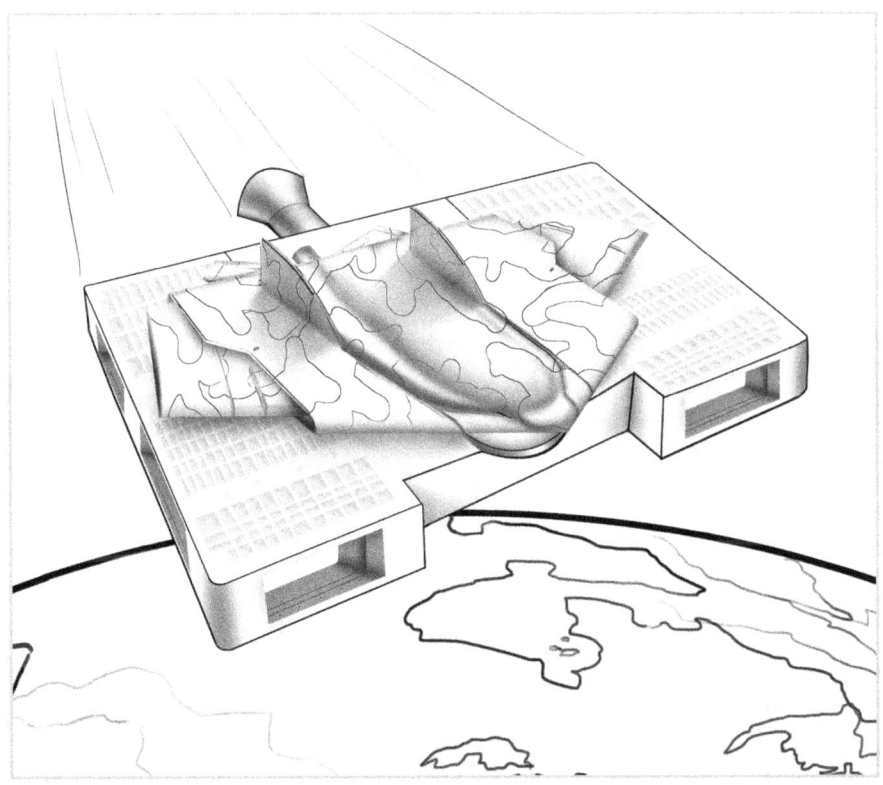

I knew my legs were surrounded by the carapace and could not collapse, but the feel of the straps was reassuring anyway.

Exactly four minutes after launch, Mother rotated the pallet 45° to the left. Twenty-seven seconds later and 1,050 klicks down the rail from Amelia Earhart Skyport, Mother released the pallet from the rail and initiated a two-minute kick thruster burn. At the end of the time, the magnetic iris sliced through the kick thruster's solid fuel stack, cutting off the burn. The pallet with *Gryphon-10* and me headed on a tangent away from the Earth at almost eight km/s on a path that passed forty-seven klicks over Fred Noonan Skyport, over Southern California, and that would intersect the 160-klick orbit on the other side of the Earth. During the acceleration phase, in addition to my leg straps, I could feel the belly band holding me securely in the pod. When the acceleration ceased, and I was in freefall, I still could feel the reassuring pressure of the belly band—kinda like Apryl's legs around my torso on Howland Island just before all this got underway.

## LEO—MANNED

To put things into perspective, I was in an elliptical orbit with perigee at eighty klicks and apogee at 160 klicks. At apogee on the opposite side of the Earth, Mother would fire the kick thruster to change my orbit from elliptical to circular. When I reached the right point in my orbit, she would rotate the pallet 180° and fire the kick thruster to slow my velocity and separate the *Gryphon-10* from the pallet. I would drop from orbit and then skip into and out of the atmosphere, slowing down each time until I was over San Diego at a manageable height and speed for landing.

As I whipped along my elliptical orbit climbing higher with each passing minute, I had a grand view of the Earth below. "Are you seeing this?" I asked.

"Roger that," Master Chief Boldt responded dryly.

"That's San Diego," I said at thirteen minutes. "Hi down there, guys!"

I told Mother to superimpose borders over my panoramic view, and two minutes later, I crossed over the Oklahoma Panhandle with a cloud cover that made it difficult to see the ground.

"Altitude one-hundred-thirty klicks," Boldt's dry voice informed me.

As I continued to gain altitude, five minutes later brilliantly lit night-time Washington, DC, swept below me.

"No time to say Hello—Good-bye…I'm flying through your nighttime sky," I sang, floating in my sling, awestruck by the speed of passing.

"Roger that," the Master Chief opined.

During the ten minutes it took to cross a darkened Atlantic, I watched lightning bolts play between towering thunderheads of a massive storm system creating a magical landscape beneath my flying carpet.

"Good morning Mauritania!" I said in my best Robin Williams imitation as I approached the West African Coast.

"Roger that. Altitude one-hundred-fifty klicks."

In the final ten minutes, I swept southeast across the Gulf of Guinea and passed into the Republic of the Congo.

"Stand by for pallet rotation," the Master Chief advised.

Dawn was breaking as I swept over Brazzaville and crossed the Congo River that bordered the Democratic Republic of the Congo. The sun glinted off the broad river surface as the city lights winked out below. The terminator swept past, and forested landscape turned from dark purple to bright green as the sun washed the blackness from the sky. As I passed over Kinshasa, the Master Chief droned, "One-hundred-sixty klicks."

Mother rotated the pallet to the proper angle and counted down the final five seconds to the circularizing burn: "Five, four, three, two, one… Initiate!"

A bright morning star flared briefly for any of the eleven-million inhabitants of Africa's third-largest city who happened to be looking overhead at that moment.

And that's when all hell broke loose.

## LEO—DISASTER

"**W**hat the fuck!" I yelped as the rear of my *Gryphon-10* pallet tilted sharply upward while the nose yawed to the right. Then the whole thing started to corkscrew while the kick thruster continued its burn. I was terrified. Almost without thinking, I manually jettisoned the kick thruster and watched it corkscrew ahead of me until it flared out. I lost it in the glare of the morning sun.

Keeping tight control of my rising panic, and very glad my belly strap held me firmly in the pod, I told Control about my problem while I deployed a tethered holocam to inspect the damage.

As I related earlier, I was in a stable orbit off to the right by 22.5° but had to get control of my tumble.

With the back end of the pallet partially melted, and a large chunk missing from my right fin, Mother gave me the bad news: "Probability of complete structure failure one hundred percent."

"Well…that's not exactly good news," I said, knowing Flight Control was listening.

"Tiger," Master Chief Boldt said, "we're working on that. While you're at it, try to conserve your oxygen."

"Control and Bird, this is Baker Socket, Baxter here. We're checking the backup bird right now. We'll send it up the skytower in about fifteen minutes."

"Baxter, this is Control. Before you send the pallet up, locate four oxygen bottles, and strap them to the pallet. Connect them to a manifold in the center of the back of the pallet. Also, send up oxygen fittings, adaptors, and any tools you think Tiger might need… anything at all." The Master Chief paused. "Oh yeah…two complete TBH boot sets." Then continued more softly. "Remember, the Skipper is up there all alone, he can't get down, and he's running out of oxygen."

"I heard that, Master Chief," I said, feeling a bit more in control. "It's not so bad as all that. Besides, the Senior Chief is already sending me everything I'll need to complete my job up here." As an afterthought, I added, "Ain't that right, Bob?"

All I heard back was a grunt.

"Mother," I said, "how close are you to fixing my tumble?"

"Approaching a solution now," she said. "Are you ready?"

"Go for it!" I said, gripping my handholds with more force than I probably needed, once again glad for the belly strap.

I sensed the nozzle moving on its gimble and felt several short rocket bursts from *Gryphon-10's* thruster—not a lot of pressure on my body, but they did push me around a bit. Mother had no way to fire forward, but somehow she managed to stop both the rotation and wobble with a small net addition to my forward velocity which meant my orbit had changed from circular to a modest ellipse.

✳

I was pretty certain that a lot was happening Earthside that was being kept from me. As the heavens above me ceased their wild gyrations, I really had nothing to do but sightsee. And I gotta tell you, it was some kind of spectacular.

By the time I was on an even keel again, Australia's nighttime west coast was just ahead of me. To the north at Coral Bay, I was told, the Australians were planning to build the Outback Loop, but as I flashed overhead, there was nothing to see of the project, just the twinkling lights of the town.

Four minutes later, as I flashed over the Great Barrier Reef Marine Park, Master Chief Boldt came up on the circuit. "Tiger, we just lifted the backup system to Amelia Earhart Skyport. We're still working out the orbital details, but we're pretty certain we can get the spare to you before you run out of oxygen."

"Thanks, Master Chief. I needed to hear that," I said with a chuckle. I had no doubt that if it were humanly possible, the guys would, at the very least, resupply me with oxygen before I ran out. And if they didn't, well…it was an analog of a parachute not opening.

As I crossed the darkened Equator five minutes later, the Master Chief brought me up to date. "We got the orbital parameters worked out, Tiger. The backup unit will rendezvous with you at the same location where the shit hit the fan in the first place. Problem is, the time is too tight to do it this orbit. You'll have to complete one more orbit to make sure you and the backup arrive over Kinshasa in exactly the same place at exactly the same time."

I was about to respond back when he added, "Yeah, we know your oxygen is tight. You might want to try breathing every other breath until the rendezvous."

"Thanks a lot, Master Chief. Seriously, what are my options?"

"We're working on that. Stand by."

"Not going anywhere, Master Chief, other than the railroad track I'm riding."

I was approaching the coast of Mexico when Flight Control got back to me. "We're sending Mother parameters to lower your total oxygen content to sixteen percent," Master Chief Boldt told me. "When you move around at all or undertake any exertion, she will boost the percentage to seventeen percent. You'll be fine, and your reduced consumption will give you the added margin you'll need when the backup gets there."

So, that was good news, sort of…it sure beat having to breathe every other breath.

As I came up on North America, my changed orbit was obvious. I passed well south of Baja California, and almost directly over the sixteenth-century town of San Luis Potosi, but it was too dark to see anything, except the lights of the town itself. Before I really had a chance to integrate the lights below me, I flashed past the Mexican coast into the Gulf about five hundred klicks south of Houston.

Houston—home to flight control of virtually every American manned space flight except mine. The phrase *Houston Flight Control* had captured my imagination since I was a small kid. And that's when it hit me.

"Master Chief Boldt, are you still there?" Silly question. Of course, he was.

"What's on your mind, Tiger?"

"Since I probably won't be landing in San Diego, can we arrange to land in the parking lot in front of the entrance to Houston Mission Control?"

I have absolutely no idea what kind of behind-the-scenes activity this innocent proposal generated, but by the time I was coming up on the West Coast of Africa for the second time, Boldt got back to me.

"It's a go, Tiger! NASA loves the idea and will do everything possible to facilitate your landing." The Master Chief actually sounded excited. "We're working out the parameters now. Generally, twenty-one-hundred klicks from Houston, you'll initiate your drop. That's just off the coast of Baja. You'll be able to see it when you initiate.

"Now…let's focus on getting you home." The Master Chief's emotionless voice had returned, so it was back to business.

Mother shifted my oxygen content to sixteen. I could tell the difference, and that made me think. The reason we were doing this is that if we didn't, I would deplete my oxygen supply before I had a chance to hook into the one they were sending me. If I ran out of oxygen before the backup pallet reached me, or even about the time it arrived, I wouldn't have enough brain power left to do what was necessary. That thought nailed it. I decided to take a nap to remain on sixteen percent as long as I physically could.

## LEO—RENDEZVOUS

Master Chief Boldt's voice jolted me awake. "Tiger, Control…Look alive! You've got work to do."

I quickly checked my heads-up readings and the map Mother had superimposed over my panoramic view. I had slept for about an hour, give or take. The backup had been launched and was on its way to our rendezvous. As the Sun rose ahead of me, I passed south of Houston, 12,000 klicks from the meet-up twenty-four minutes hence.

"Tiger, time to do what you practiced in Max."

"I practiced a lot of things in Max…most of them got me killed!" I wasn't really grumpy, but my sense of humor was lagging behind me in orbit.

"Tiger, you need to extricate yourself from the *Gryphon*. Gotta be ready for whatever might happen at rendezvous."

"Roger, Master Chief. I'm working on that right now." Boldt was more than right. If things went exactly as planned, my pallet and the replacement would end up side-by-side. All I would need to do is slip out of the damaged *Gryphon-10* into the replacement, and then ride it out for about forty-three minutes to the drop point. But real life has a habit of interfering with the best-laid plans. I had one shot at the rendezvous. I needed every advantage I could get.

Time to undress. I manually released the seal around the pod cover. A cloud of moisturized air escaped, forming an expanding halo around the pallet. I activated the mechanism that opened the *Gryphon-10* pod cover like a clamshell carrying me with it. My arms and hands were free, so I loosened the waistband and then undid the leg straps. I had nineteen minutes left to think about all the things that could go wrong.

"Tiger, Control…The backup will approach you from below to your rear. Its differential velocity should be very small both along your orbital axis and your vertical axis. You should see it in about five minutes."

"I'm lookin' hard, Master Chief, trust me!"

## LEO—MISS

Looking down against the bright Atlantic surface for a small approaching object is not exactly what I had trained for, but you better believe I concentrated more than I ever had before.

I picked it up three or four minutes later—I sort of lost track of time I was concentrating so hard. "I see the pallet, Master Chief!"

"That's a bit early," he answered. "It's gonna go right past you… but pretty slow." He paused. "Give me an angle from the base of your pallet."

I sighted and let Mother do the math. "Ten-and-a-half degrees, Master Chief."

"Yeah, we see it. That's a problem. Should be about seven to eight degrees. Sucker's going to pass you at about one-point-four meters-per-second. What's the pallet's relative bearing drift?"

I watched it for a few seconds. "It's pulling off to my right…"

"Wait one," the Master Chief said. "I'm patching NASA through."

"This is Flight Control Houston, Tiger. We got you and the approaching pallet on high-resolution radar. You are at three-hundred meters and closing at one-point-four meters-per-second, decreasing. At CPA (*that's*

*Closest Point of Approach for you landlubbers*), the pallet will be one hundred meters off your starboard side at ten-point-four degrees above your plane, one-point-two meters-per-second relative velocity."

"Mother, time of CPA?" I asked.

"Three-minutes-and-fifty-seconds."

I thought about tethering myself to my pallet, but considering the forces involved, I decided I would be better off on my own under TBH propulsion. After all, 1.4 m/sec was about walking speed. I should be able to catch the pallet just a football field away.

"Mother, give me angle and time to commence personal burn to rendezvous with pallet." Believe it or not, she actually understood that.

"Two-minutes-and-three-seconds; heading zero-nine-zero relative; ten-degree up-angle. You will need to correct continuously as you traverse."

I had less than a minute. As Mother counted down the last few seconds, I said, "Captain, Master Chief…wish me luck!" I oriented myself and tapped both big toes…and whispered, *There's no place like home!*

Mother set my heads-up display to show the pallet carrying the spare *Gryphon-10* on its projected path, myself on my projected path, and the rendezvous point. I concentrated on keeping my path intersecting the rendezvous point. I was a little low and to the right. I bent both knees just a bit and moved my left leg outward a fraction. As the points closed, I got ready and then tapped both toes to shut down the TBH boots. As we closed still five meters apart, I tucked and rolled, pointing my feet at the pallet. Two taps with each toe—on and off, and I grabbed the pallet.

"Nice job!" the Master Chief commented. "Now buckle in! You got a circularizing burn coming up in a minute."

He didn't say *Hustle!*, but I heard it in his voice. The *Gryphon-10* was a hardy beast, but it was not designed to take acceleration with the clamshell open. It took me thirty-five seconds to open it, lie face down, and shut it over me. I was not strapped to anything, so I grabbed my hand controls, braced my knees against the pod, and held on.

"On my mark," Master Chief Boldt said. "Three, two, one…fire!"

I don't know what I was expecting, but the acceleration caught me by surprise. About ten seconds or so of something less than one-gee, and that was it.

"You're good to go," the Master Chief informed me.

I couldn't have increased my oxygen percentage to 21% if I had wanted to. I was quite literally on my last couple of breaths. I rolled out of the clamshell and quickly hooked the oxygen manifold to my backpack and recharged my tanks. There was no need to inform Control.

I opened the clamshell and pressed against the pod cover. I strapped my legs to the pod. I tightened the broad waist strap, placed my arms at my sides, and then closed and sealed the Gryphon-10. As I crossed the east coast of Africa, I was ready to go.

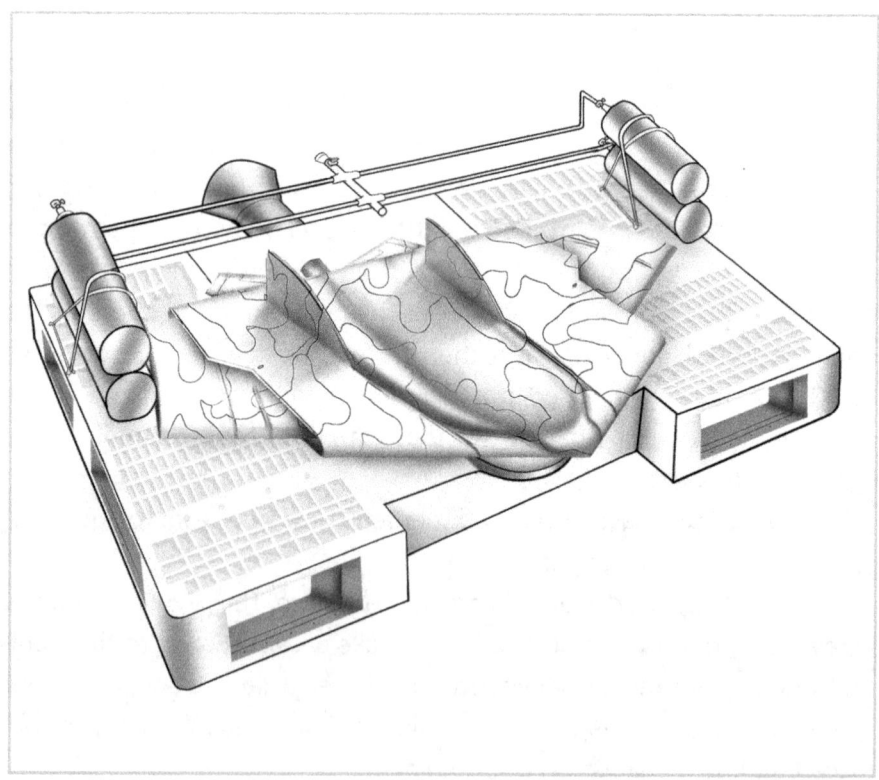

## LEO—ORBIT SHIFT

By now, I had sufficient oxygen to make several trips around the globe, but my bladder bag was filling, and I had already tested the capacity of my astronaut diapers. It was definitely time to go home.

"Tiger, this is Control." It was the Master Chief again.

"What's up, Master Chief?"

"Nothin ain't easy," he said. "Your successful rendezvous and burn were not *entirely* successful. You can't make Houston on your present path."

"Well…sheeit!" I said. I really wanted to do that landing. "Master Chief," I said after a minute of thought, "check with Houston, but I think we might be able to adjust my orbit. I got a bunch of pressurized oxygen up here with the manifold pointed to the rear. I got the nearly full kick thruster and my TBH boots with two spare sets."

"Well…" Master Chief Boldt was obviously skeptical.

"I can do another orbit or two if we have to. We still have half-a-day before night sets over Houston."

"Tiger, this is Houston Flight Control. I need a complete inventory of what you have up there. SWIC Flight Control, give me the mass and dimension parameters for the items on Tiger's inventory."

My part was easy. "The pallet with a partially used kick thruster; four oxygen tanks, just an RCH under six-hundred-eighty atmospheres; the TBH boots I'm wearing and two fully charged extra pairs; my spacesuit with fully charged pack; the *Gryphon-10* with fully charged thruster." I also listed the hand tools Senior Chief Baxter had attached to the pallet.

"Houston…" It was the Master Chief. "I'm calling you on a secure line."

I knew what this was all about. NASA is a sieve when it comes to classified material, and *Gryphon-10* carried a classification above Top Secret. Capt. Nelson would be bending some ears at NASA to ensure the confidentiality of our project.

❋

At SWIC headquarters, all available personnel assembled in the North Island hanger. They had one purpose, one goal: quickly create a mockup of my pallet and link it to NASA by holocam. Our best and NASA's best people would be working with the mockup to find a real-time solution to my predicament.

It took them a bit over a half-hour. They uploaded instructions for Mother and walked me through my part of the operation.

I shifted my oxygen backup to the outside right tank. I modified the oxygen manifold so that by opening just one valve, 680 atm of oxygen would provide thrust to the rear of the pallet, and I attached a stiff wire to the valve handle that reached to my left-hand location outside the carapace. I replaced my TBH boots with a fresh pair and prepared to angle myself with my feet pointing in a direction specified by Mother, varying the angle in real time as she directed. The combined team decided not to employ the kick thruster because I would need it for deorbiting. They decided not to use the *Gryphon-10's* thruster, but to hold it in reserve for my drop. That was fine by me.

To sum up, I would use thrust generated by the oxygen tanks and whatever my TBH boots would produce. As I came up to a point about 500 klicks northwest of Jarvis Island, I would initiate the "burn" to shift my orbit left by a couple of degrees. The exact time, duration, and direction of thrust would be determined in real-time by Houston's Flight Control Computer talking directly with Mother.

I had about a half-hour to worry about what would happen if this maneuver didn't work. Worst-case scenario would find me ditching somewhere in the Gulf of Mexico, with rescue coming by air or sea, depending on how far from civilization I hit the drink. Did I say *worst-case-scenario*? Actually, I could think of several that were much worse, but being an optimist, I chose not to consider *not making it* as an option.

My personal time sense must have been out of kilter, because what seemed a minute or so later, Mother announced five minutes to the correction.

I remained inside the *Gryphon-10*, but with the seal cracked and the wire in my hand. Mother had already changed the pallet orientation, so we were pointed about 10° to the left of our direction of travel. Houston had calculated the expected amount of thrust the oxygen bottles would generate, but there were way too many variables to be certain. I was prepared to extract myself from the *Gryphon-10* on a moment's notice to add the thrust of my TBH boots to our acceleration profile.

Mother commenced her countdown: "Ten, nine… three, two, one…fire!"

I pulled the wire, and wouldn't you know, it slipped from the valve handle without opening the valve. "Fuck it all!" I said while I slid out of the carapace. With my left hand, I grabbed a carabiner with a two-meter safety line attached to my utility belt and slapped it onto a tie-down to the left of the wingsuit while I swung back to the manifold and twisted the valve with my right. A stream of oxygen looking every bit like a small rocket exhaust shot out the hole in the manifold. The pallet shot forward, popping the *Gryphon-10* pod cover open and jerking my utility belt, dragging me behind the pallet with a pull that had to be approaching one-gee.

If the acceleration damaged the *Gryphon*-10 hinge, I might not make it back. I tried to pull myself hand-over-hand along the safety line, but the acceleration was too strong. I had only one option: I tapped both toes. The TBH boots didn't cancel out the acceleration, but they gave me enough advantage to do the hand-over-hand thing. Even so, it took me several seconds. When I got to the pod cover, I tapped my toes to shut down the jets, wrapped a loop of safety line over the open upper end, pulled it down and cinched it to a tie-down on the other side. Then I held on for the duration.

Finally, Mother ordered, "Secure the burn."

I knew what she meant and didn't argue her terminology. Without letting the safety line go, I reached back and shut the valve. The stream of oxygen dissipated, and everything seemed to return to normal. I unwrapped the safety line from the pod cover and carefully exercised the hinge. So far as I could tell, there was no damage.

As I removed and stowed the safety line, I queried: "What's the status, Master Chief? Did we make it, or am I going to tread water in the Gulf?"

"This is Houston Flight Control, Tiger. We do not fully understand your *Gryphon-10* parameters, but your new orbit passes directly over Trinity Bay."

"That's a go," Master Chief Boldt said without formally identifying himself. "By damn, that's a go!"

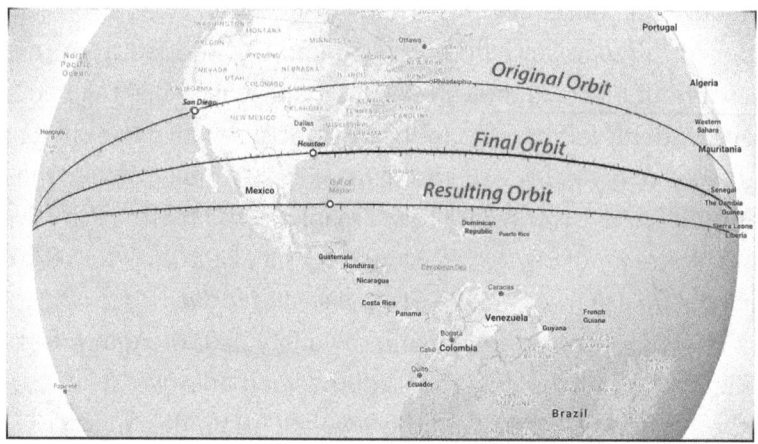

**Figure 1:** *Orbital paths as they pass over the U.S. and Mexico of the Original Orbit, the Resulting Orbit after the accident, and the Final Orbit following the correction.*

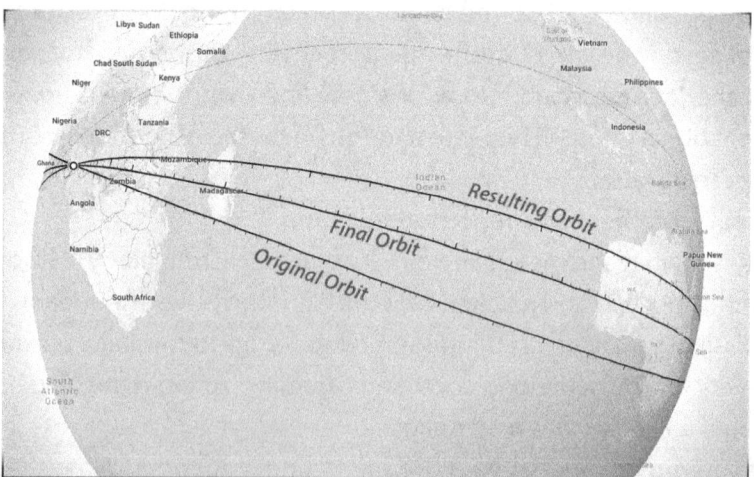

**Figure 2:** *Orbital paths from Kinshasa to Australia of the Original Orbit, the Resulting Orbit after the accident, and the Final Orbit following the correction.*

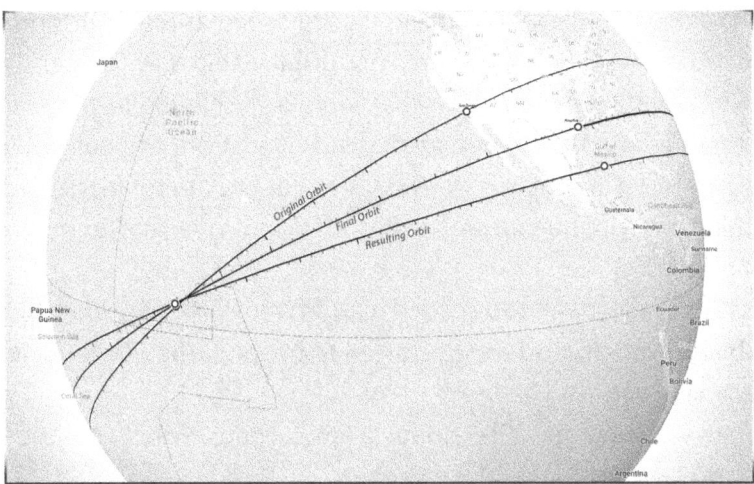

**Figure 3:**   *Orbital paths over the Pacific of the Original Orbit, the Resulting Orbit after the accident, and the Final Orbit following the correction over the Pacific.*

## LEO—MANNED DROP

The first thing Mother did was rotate the pallet 180° with the launch pouch gyro while I secured myself into the *Gryphon*-10. This was the real thing. Once Mother initiated the deorbiting burn, there was no turning back. My heads-up display told me I was 400 klicks off Baja California. I knew the burn would commence right around 200 klicks—I had about thirty seconds.

"Godspeed!" Master Chief Boldt said as Mother initiated the burn twenty-eight seconds later.

After the two longest minutes of my life, Mother cut the kick thruster and rotated everything back, so I was pointed in my direction of travel. I felt a sharp jolt.

"Pallet separation," Mother announced. "Forward velocity six-eight-hundred meters-per-second."

I think I may have briefly seen the pallet fall away, but *Gryphon-10* was heading toward the horizon at 6,800 m/sec while accelerating toward the ocean at 9.8 m/sec². Fat chance I actually saw it. Mother had set a timer when she separated the pallet. The digits flashed at the right side of my display. At the two-minute mark, my display told me Copper Canyon was sixty klicks below—*Barranca del Cobre*—in Chihuahua, Mexico. I had been there a couple of times, even wingsuited from the balcony of the Divisadero Hotel. It took me three days to get back to the ridge. But right now, things were happening too fast, and I didn't have time for reminiscing or sightseeing.

As I approached the 150-second mark at forty klicks, *Gryphon-10* began to grab atmosphere, and things started to heat up. The Master Chief said, "Talk to me, Tiger!"

"Suit's warming up…I'll continue a few seconds more…"

At 160 seconds, I said, "Now, Mother!"

Mother had already gimbled the rocket nozzle to push the stern down and adjusted the wing torque controls to optimize my return to space. I felt weight return as I rocketed upward. Then Mother cut the burn and announced, "Forward velocity five-zero-eight-five meters-per-second, net forward transfer nine-two-one kilometers."

I watched the timer reset as Mother said, "Vertical motion zero on my mark…Mark!"

Although Mach numbers don't really matter at this altitude, we started out at Mach 20, and as we began to grab air sixty-four klicks above Copper Canyon, we were still near Mach 18 and frigging hot. When Mother fired the rocket at forty klicks and made slight adjustments to *Gryphon-10's* control surfaces, the wingsuit headed back out of the atmosphere, but 1,500 m/sec slower. We were down to Mach 15 as we commenced the second dip.

Other than the landscape below, I really could tell no meaningful difference between the first and second dips. We hit Mach 9 sixty-five klicks above Big Bend off to my left a bit. After we climbed back out of the atmosphere, we were down to Mach 5, and I let out a whoop.

"You okay?" Boldt wanted to know.

"Yeah! This is cool stuff. I think I could do this without Mother's assistance. The heat tells you when to pop, and physics does everything else."

"Roger that," the Master Chief said, "but Mother will get you to your destination. Without her, you could end up anywhere."

He was right, of course. But I had this thing down…I knew it in my bones.

The next drop put me at forty klicks altitude, 100 klicks west of Houston at sixty m/sec.

Immediately, I was in familiar territory, no different really from my Fred Noonan Skyport jump, except there was land below instead of water.

"Are you guys getting this?" I asked with a level of excitement that even I could hear.

"Piece of cake, Tiger," the Master Chief drawled. "Nothin' you ain't done before. Keep the chatter comin'!"

At this altitude and speed, I had virtually full control of *Gryphon-10*. I brought myself as horizontal as possible and headed for Trinity Bay.

✳

"What's the air traffic situation?" I asked.

"NASA'S dealing with that," the Master Chief said.

As he spoke, two NASA jets pulled up, about 200 meters off each side. Even though they couldn't see my face, each pilot gave me a friendly salute.

"Air traffic is being kept away from your path," The Master Chief told me. "Come in about a thousand meters above Trinity Bay, and then follow Mother's display." Then the Master Chief added, "Oh yeah, we've cleared the parking lot for you."

*Shouldn't have been necessary, really,* I thought. *The* Gryphon-10 *fits in a standard parking lot driveway, but why not.*

As I arrived about a thousand meters above central Trinity Bay, my escorts departed with a wing-waggle. I turned left, and Mother laid out a perfectly clear path right to Houston Flight Control's front door. I was still twenty-eight klicks out, but my path was straight in. I was doing about thirty m/sec, or about 100 km/hr. At that speed, it would take me fifteen minutes, but I would hit the ground half-way there unless I used my booster. And then I had to slow down to walking speed for my landing.

## HOUSTON FLIGHT CONTROL—LANDING

With full tanks, I could go a hundred horizontal klicks on the booster. I had only about a quarter of my fuel left, but that was more than sufficient to travel the remaining twenty-eight klicks. This was going to be fun.

I hit the booster for a few seconds while shedding altitude, glided for a bit, and gave it another boost. I was 500 meters away from the parking lot and 100 meters above the trees. A small welcoming crowd stood at the door and across the lot two lanes away. That's when the landing skid of a local news chopper clipped my right fin.

"Where the fuck did that guy come from?" I yelped as I began to lose control of the *Gryphon-10*. A hundred meters is a long way to fall. People scattered in all directions, seeking cover.

"Mother, can you compensate?" I asked.

Mother immediately ignited the booster and drove me skyward for a hundred meters while she experimented with different wing and fin control settings until she found a combination that seemed to work.

"Bring me down in front of the main door," I told Mother.

"This one?" She illuminated the entrance on my display.

"Yeah, that one," I said.

As I slowly spiraled down, the crowd moved closer. I was still about two meters above the pavement moving forward at about one m/sec when a bicycle inexplicably pushed through the crowd directly below me. I don't know what that NASA nerd was thinking, but it was pretty obvious that— even though his head was in the clouds—he had not seen me. I could do absolutely nothing except pull my nose up sharply while retracting my tail.

The *Gryphon-10* is supposed to land on its belly. I didn't do that. I was retracting my tail when I struck the pavement with my booster and fell forward right on top of the rider. I think that was the first indication he had that I was there.

The rider tumbled to the left as his bike flew to the right. He staggered to his feet, staring at the *Gryphon-10* in utter astonishment. As he picked himself up from the pavement, I unsealed the carapace, and the pod cover flipped to vertical carrying me with it. Still in my spacesuit, I unstrapped myself, stepped away from the *Gryphon-10*, and released my transparent helmet, and then held out my hand to the cyclist. He looked me over in total disbelief, and then removed his helmet and shook my hand.

The crowd cheered, and everyone rushed me, clapping me on the back, shaking my hand, and even kissing me—yep, I got three very welcoming kisses from three more than passable ladies who probably each had more brains than my entire SWIC-3 command combined.

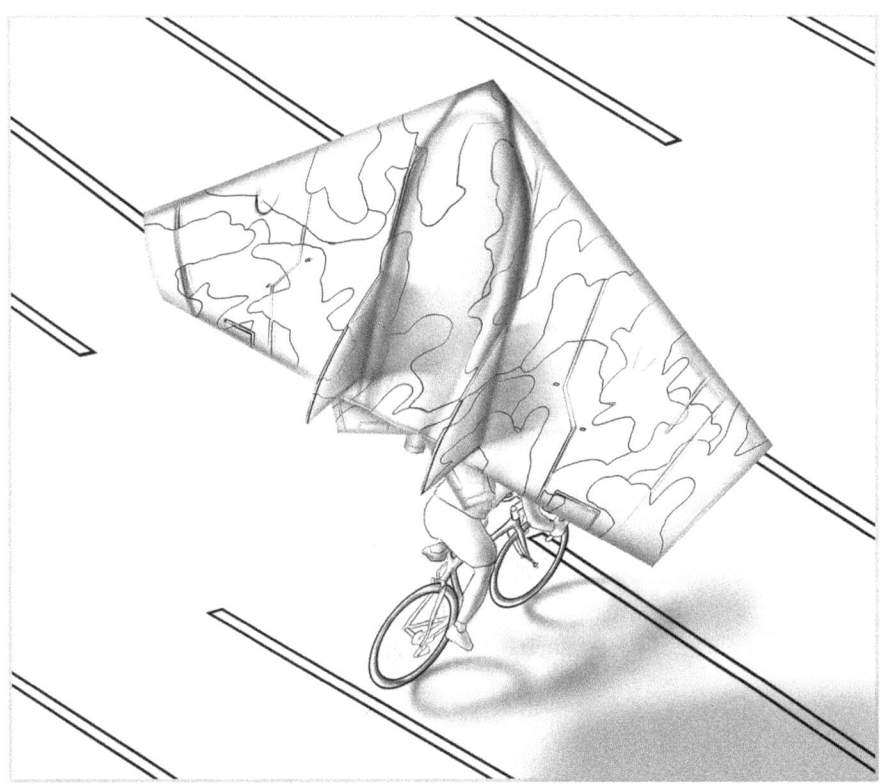

## DAEDALUS II—FINALE

Secrets will out, and this one did—rather quickly. I spent a bit of quality time with one of the kissers. The cyclist and I tossed a couple of brews. NASA flew *Gryphon-10* and me back to San Diego where we all celebrated again.

I'm sure you know the rest of the story. Obviously, I survived, and then I survived my second fifteen minutes of fame. My *Gryphon-10* hangs alongside my old *Gryphon-7* in the Smithsonian, but you know that, as well.

Every SWIC-3 team member has now accomplished an LEO drop—without NASA's help, by-the-way. Right now, we're working on a group drop that will simulate dropping into a combat zone. I'll let you know when that finally happens.

# PLEASE POST A REVIEW
# FOR DAEDALUS LEO

## ON

## AMAZON.COM AND GOODREADS.COM

I really appreciate you posting a review on Amazon and Goodreads. Posting to Amazon.com is intuitive. To post a review on Goodreads.com, click on this link, or go to their website, and become a member if you are not already one. Search for *Daedalus*, and click on the "Want to read" button under the image of *Daedalus*. Indicate that you have read *Daedalus* and then you will be able to post a review. Thank you very much for going through this effort!

# EXCERPT FROM THE FIRST CHAPTER OF: SLINGSHOT

by

### Robert G. Williscroft

## EQUATORIAL PACIFIC—SOUTHEAST OF BAKER ISLAND

Margo stopped kicking her feet as the ominous gray shapes flashed into her peripheral view. Long, tawny hair floated past her head as her feet dropped below her slim, brightly clad body. She took a deep breath and floated slightly upward. A hint of fear crept into her mind as she turned toward three gray, sleek predators cruising just inside the limit of her vision, about twenty-five meters away.

A gentle touch on her shoulder startled her. She turned to see Alex Regent tapping the depth reading on his dive-console with his index finger. Margo reached down and grasped her console, turning it so she could read her depth: twenty-five meters. She had drifted upward five meters since seeing the sharks.

Margo exhaled angrily and let some air out of her breathing bag. She knew better than to lose track of her depth. Out there, her life depended on a constant awareness of exactly how deep she was. Together she and Alex sank back to thirty meters. Off to their right, the three gray shapes drifted with them. Would she ever get used to it, she thought, as she released a bit of air into her bag to stop her descent.

"Alex," she said.

There was no response.

"Alex!" She tapped the back of her console several times.

"Alex!" Nothing but silence.

Alex placed himself in front of Margo and looked into her facemask. With his right hand, he formed a circle with thumb and forefinger. His three other fingers extended straight up.

Margo returned the sign indicating she was all right while nodding vigorously. Then she pointed to her ear and lifted her console, tapping the back. Alex fumbled at his ear and then tapped his console, and then shook his head.

*Great*, Margo thought, *EFCom is busted just when we really need it. Not busted,* she corrected herself, *just a submerged antenna.* She pointed to the three menacing shapes off to her right. Alex turned and scanned around them. Above and just behind them the blue-painted hull of their boat bobbed in the gentle waves. About twenty meters ahead of them hung a smooth, horizontal fluorescent orange tube about one meter in diameter. To the left, it stretched into the gloom; to the right, it angled downward. The fluorescent tube was attached to a slender cable angling up to the shadow of a buoy just beneath the surface to their right. Alex turned back toward Margo, making an exaggerated shrug.

Margo reached for her dive-console again and pressed a button located prominently on its face. The three sharks turned and commenced a meandering movement toward the two divers. Their front fins extended stiffly downward at about forty-five degrees. Their backs arched slightly, and their blunt snouts moved back and forth as they approached.

Margo felt her hair stand up on the nape of her neck. She turned to Alex and motioned him to her side. Alex withdrew a telescoped baton from its holder at his waist and extended it to its full one-and-a-half-meter length. He checked the safety lever near its handle, and with his thumb he flicked the lever so it pointed forward. As the sharks drew nearer, he held the stick out in front of him, pointed in their direction. Margo glanced around them again and pushed her console button once more. Alex waved the stick about slowly and then steadied up on the nearest of the three menacing monsters.

Suddenly, with blurring speed, the nearest shark attacked. Alex struck out with his stick, the jolt of its impact rocking him backward. A sharp crack was followed by a hissing sound as carbon dioxide rushed into the shark's body. In the same moment, flashes of silvery-black streaked from several directions. One of the remaining sharks was struck broadside by a dolphin's blunt nose. In a flash, it disappeared.

The animal Alex had injected rolled on its side and began a crazed, uncontrolled spiral toward the surface thirty meters above them. On its way up, it was hit several times by charging dolphins. It expired of massive embolisms before reaching fifteen meters. In the melee, the third shark vanished.

Margo reached out for Alex, grabbed a handful of breathing bag, and pulled him close to her. She placed the flat of her full-facemask against his and looked deeply into his eyes, as close to a kiss as she could come under the circumstances. Even down here, they were deep blue. Several bubbles escaped from the positive pressure maintained inside their masks and shimmered their way toward the surface, expanding rapidly as they rose.

*Like an old-time scuba diver*, Margo thought, watching the rising silvery spheres. Instinctively she checked the volume in her breathing bag and glanced at the gauge on her tiny, ultra-high-pressure air flask. She found she was holding her breath, and as she felt the need to breathe, a gentle pressure developed against her back. She pulled back and turned to confront a two-and-a-half-meter-long dolphin nudging her from behind.

It was one of four that had responded to her sonic signal—George, her favorite. The other three dolphins crowded in around the neoprene and nylon suited divers, jostling each other for attention. Margo rubbed the head dome of each and indicated to Alex that he should do the same. Then the two of them turned their attention back to the tube suspended in front of them.

Alex swam to the angled portion and began to search along the tube's length, descending slowly. Margo dropped her arm from George's neck and kicked in Alex's direction, keeping him in sight, but staying between him and the surface. The four cetaceans arrowed toward the surface and grabbed a gulp of air, then settled back down, playfully cycling between Alex and Margo, gently jostling them. About thirty minutes later, Alex motioned Margo to join him. She released a bubble of air from her bag and dropped down beside him. Her console showed a depth of fifty meters. Alex pointed to a five-centimeter rip in the bottom curve of the tube's fluorescent covering.

Margo reached into a deep pocket located on the left leg of her suit and withdrew a role of patching tape. Alex stretched the edges of the tear, and Margo applied a strip of self-sealing tape along the opening. Then she located a small pneumatic valve on the top of the tube and attached a hose from her spare air tank. On a signal from Alex, she released air into the tube, forcing water out through a one-way valve on the underside. She stopped when bubbles escaped from the lower valve.

As the tube rose slowly, Margo held on, keeping track of their progress on her console. They stopped rising when the gauge read thirty meters. Margo felt the tube—it was taut and solid. She tapped the back of her console, listening for the faint rush of sound in her ears. Nothing. She pointed to the back of her console and then her ear, and shook her head. Alex offered another of his exaggerated underwater shrugs and grinned, although the only part of the grin she could see was his crinkled eyes. She grinned back and pointed toward the suspension buoy and their boat, making an angled upward sign with her free hand. Alex nodded, checked his console, and they both headed back, slowly rising as they swam.

Margo saw Alex check his console from time to time, making certain they kept below the ever-changing ceiling limit it calculated for him. Since she had remained shallower than Alex for most of the dive, she knew she would be safe following his lead. She looked around at the four dolphins. Her earlier fright was gone, and she simply enjoyed George's protective nearness and the playful bumps and nudges from the others.

On the surface finally, Alex dropped his facemask down around his neck, fully inflated his bag and grinned at Margo. "Close call down there!"

Margo shoved her facemask down and patted the glistening snout that appeared in front of her. "Thanks, George. I love you too."

The dolphin mewed a pleased response, lifted his body out of the water and backed away, chattering as he went. The other three animals circled at and below the surface, keeping watch over their human charges.

"What happened to the EFCom?" Margo asked. "I expected it to come back online as soon as the antenna surfaced."

"Broken antenna wire, I imagine," Alex answered.

"Storm damage, I'm sure," said Margo, as they turned and headed toward the waiting vessel.

"Probably," agreed Alex. "But that wasn't a burst seam," he added.

"Yeah, maybe the sinking tube snapped the wire."

Actually, tube flotation chambers flooded on a regular basis. They had patched a full ten percent of them since the project started. But it was a bit unusual to find a rip on the tube bottom, and the Electrostatic Field Communication ("EFCom") transceivers on the buoys almost always survived.

※

The EFCom buoy nearest the tear had ceased transmitting, and the buoys on either side of the tear had signaled their departure from datum a day earlier. Alex had opted to employ an electrostatic field communication system, because of its clear underwater signal transmission capability that was independent of acoustic conditions, since it didn't rely on sound transmission through the water. Every buoy, each skimmer and floater, and every diver was outfitted with one of the small EFCom transceivers.

Alex had inspected the non-transmitting buoy personally during an overflight from Jarvis Island. There was nothing visible on the two kilometers of surface between the buoys; they were closer together, but not so that it was visible to the eye. Nevertheless, the remaining 1,828-odd buoy-suspended kilometers of tube were stressing from the downward pull of the waterlogged section. The buoy near the tear was several meters underwater.

Suspended inside the flotation tube were two virtually impervious, lightweight, hose-like tubes, each about six centimeters in diameter, called vacuum sheaths. Two shallow channels jutted out from the bottom of each vacuum sheath, filled with electronically controlled suspending magnets. Magnetically suspended inside each vacuum sheath was a five-centimeter tube of segmented soft iron officially called the rotor, but more popularly known as the ribbon, so named from the earliest conceptions back in the 1980s of the Launch Loop inventor, Keith Lofstrom. Alex was eager to check continuity readings to make certain the vacuum sheaths had not breached. They were not yet evacuated, but seawater entry at this stage would seriously delay the entire project. If the EFCom had not crapped out, the tests would already be underway.

Alex glanced ahead at Margo Jackson, cavorting with her four dolphins as they made their leisurely way back to the waiting boat. His field engineer in charge of underwater construction was a remarkable female. Nearly as tall as his own 183 centimeters, her model's slender figure, encased in electric-blue nylon-covered neoprene, seemed to lack feminine curves. He knew differently, of course, having joined her bikini-clad person from time to time for morning swims since the project began over two years ago.

The project—Alex had lived with it for three years before actual construction began. Longer, actually, if you considered dreams—since before the incredible, worldwide bi-millennial celebration when he still was a young boy.

There was the nearly simultaneous publication in America and England of practically identical ideas in 1985. Paul Birch published an article in *The Journal of the British Interplanetary Society*, while in America Keith Lofstrom published his article in a supplement to *The Journal of the Astronautical Sciences*, he recalled. Nobody could agree on the names: Skyrail, Launch Loop, Beanstalk. There were others, but the idea is what counted, the sky-shaking idea that you don't need rockets to get into space.

Newspapers were full of explanations three-and-a-half years ago when the aging president of a computer software giant made the announcement. He would funnel a significant portion of company profits into the consortium. Space travel would become as commonplace and inexpensive as the personal computers his pioneering work had made possible. He went on to outline the easy-to-understand concept.

Imagine a water hose streaming water in a parabolic arch. Deflect the water and funnel it back to the start through a pump, creating a closed system. Make the stream strong enough and the hose light enough, and the entire structure will support itself—the water holding up the hose structure. Now, replace the water with a thin, closed-loop pipe of segmented soft iron. Make it 5,000 kilometers around and accelerate it to orbital velocity with gigantic linear induction motors from two points on the equator 2,000 kilometers apart. The center section of the structure, including both the outgoing and return legs of the loop, will rise to about eighty kilometers above the Earth. Supply access to the upstream end in space with a Kevlar-hung elevator, and you can launch capsules by magnetically coupling them to the rapidly moving pipe of iron.

*Slingshot*, they called it. The greatest engineering undertaking in the history of the world, they said.

As the on-scene project manager, Alex was responsible for getting the job done, on schedule, on budget. He was building a gossamer structure over 2,500 kilometers long, a frail spider web, completely invisible when viewed from more than a few kilometers. Alex grinned wryly. All *Slingshot* really consisted of was a fancy evacuated tube, a flexible iron pipe, four linear drivers and their power sources, some guy wires, and a couple of elevators. Put that way it seemed simple enough. But, of course, it wasn't simple at all, and for all his skill and engineering competence, and despite surface appearances, deep down Alex was not entirely sure that he could make it happen.

Margo and Alex climbed up the ladder and onto *Skimmer One's* bobbing fantail. This was one of two skimmers on the project—twelve-meter-long surface-effect boats that looked more like a floating aircraft than a traditional motorboat. They were capable of 200 knots, skimming about one-and-a-half meters over the wave tops. They had a small open fantail, just large enough for a couple of divers to doff their gear. Being on the fantail when the skimmer was on its cushion was more than dangerous, and was strictly prohibited throughout the project.

Alex signaled to the waiting coxswain, and they got underway for Baker, plowing through the water while Alex and Margo remained exposed. He and Margo stood near the stern railing and removed their dripping skins. Alex looked back at the buoys, now presumably in their proper places.

"How many more times?" Alex looked quizzically at Margo.

"Who knows?" She glanced back at the bobbing buoys. "We have repair people available at both ends. We shouldn't be doing this ourselves, you know." She turned and looked directly at Alex. "What do you think—weather or sabotage?"

Alex shrugged and tossed the spent carbon dioxide cartridge from his shark stick in the general direction of the cavorting dolphins. "I wanted to see for myself, and I still don't know. Does it matter? We can't patrol the entire eighteen-hundred-twenty-eight-kilometer length anyway."

"What are we dealing with?" Margo asked. "You don't get out here in a rowboat."

"We're two thousand wet klicks from any kind of civilization," Alex said. "At minimum, that's a large motor-yacht or even an ocean sailer—you know, one of those we maybe can afford when this job is done." He sighed. "We're dealing with lots of money and someone with a major bitch."

He looked into her green eyes.

"Just keep my tubes at depth." His blue eyes flashed, and he turned toward the cockpit to radio his orders to test pipe continuity.

✷

Margo dropped her eyes at his challenge. For the thousandth time, she asked herself if she had bitten off more than she could chew with this assignment. Was it her fault that the flotation chambers kept ripping? Was she missing something important? Was she copping out to imply there might have been sabotage? And yet, Alex seemed to agree that it might be sabotage. When she joined the project two years ago, the newspapers had acclaimed her as the ideal role model for the new twenty-first-century woman. At times that burden lay heavily on her shoulders, as it did now, she reflected.

It was a vast responsibility, and there was no way one person actually could control all of it at once. How Alex handled the weight of the entire project awed her, but she was careful never to let him know.

Margo watched Alex step into the cockpit. He was tall and slender, richly tanned from his constant outdoor work. She felt a softness well up inside her, a gentle warmth spreading out from the pit of her stomach. She bit her lower lip and turned angrily to lean on the after-railing.

None of that, she chided herself. This assignment was too important, and the stakes too high, to let any kind of emotion intrude. As she entered the cabin and sealed the port, the skipper switched modes, and pressurized air quickly filled the hard-sided skirt. In moments the skimmer lifted out of the water, except for the port and starboard skirts that protruded about a meter into the waves. Within seconds, high-pressure water nozzles jetted water from the end of each skirt, and within thirty seconds *Skimmer One* was approaching 200 knots.

As *Skimmer One* headed into the afternoon sun, trailing an arrow-straight wake of white foam, Margo stood looking aft through the sealed port, remembering her instinctive sharing, and their underwater kiss following the fright of nearly becoming shark food. She shook off the sensation and busied herself with putting away their diving equipment. But a hint of a smile remained on her lips as they shot over the surface, finally settling back onto the water as they entered the small protected artificial harbor on the west side of Baker Island, just south of a shallow reef that went dry at low tide.

*You have just been reading from Chapter One of Slingshot,*
*the 1st book in **The Starchild** Trilogy, Robert Williscroft's*
*exciting Science Fiction trilogy. **To read the rest***
***of this book, click here:** **Slingshot.***

# WORDS OF PRAISE
# FOR SLINGSHOT

*Slingshot* does for the launch loop what Arthur C. Clarke's *The Fountains of Paradise* or Sheffield's *Web Between the Worlds* did for the space elevator. Again, Williscroft delivers a great mix of hard science fiction and action.

— **Alastair Mayer**
**Author of the *T-Space Series***

Robert Williscroft deftly crafts an energetic story around a phenomenal technological development just over the horizon: the space launch loop. The technical detail woven into this story is an education unto itself. But don't assume that Williscroft chooses raw infodump over story—*Slingshot* is an adventure that pulls you in, gives you characters that are engaging, and invites you to follow them through their challenges. What Williscroft has done in *Slingshot* is no easy task—he has balanced the *hard* aspect of science fiction with the character portrayals that those who despise that very *hard* science fiction beg for. The last decade has seen impressive leaps in the theoretical work toward the launch loop—this book couldn't come too soon! And you won't be able to keep from reading all the way to the end. Williscroft's art continues to be praise-worthy!

— **Jason D. Batt, *100 Year Starship***
**Author of *The Tales of Dreamside series***

I've been a fan of Robert Williscroft's books for a while now. They're action-packed and filled with all kinds of interesting, real-world information. *Slingshot* fits right in.

*Slingshot* is about the development of an earth-bound spaceport in which spaceships are taken 80 kilometers above the Earth by elevator and hurled onto their trajectory by a very fast moving ribbon of soft iron. It is much easier, cheaper, and cleaner to launch spaceships from here due to the rarified atmosphere. This concept may be a reality someday. The book begins with a foreword by Keith Lofstrom, the originator of this concept called the "launch loop."

Learning about the launch loop is the most interesting aspect of this novel. Williscroft's descriptions of the construction techniques, its operations, and the benefits for space travel are absolutely fascinating. The book takes place about thirty years in the future, and I could easily see such a project becoming a reality in that time.

The plot of the novel is driven by the development and construction of the project, which is being threatened by ill-informed environmentalists bent on destroying the project. The launch loop is far greener than the current method of launching vehicles into space, but a sinister power has misled the environmentalists into believing that sabotaging the launch loop is saving the planet. Meanwhile, the sinister power is protecting its own economic interests.

As usual, Williscroft has created a cast of interesting and driven characters. The book is a fascinating read, and you are guaranteed not only to learn a lot, but to dream about the future of space travel.

— **Marc Weitz, Past President**
**The Los Angeles Adventurers' Club**

*Click here to read* **Slingshot**

# ABOUT THE AUTHOR

**D**r. Robert G. Williscroft served twenty-three years in the U.S. Navy and the National Oceanic and Atmospheric Administration (NOAA). He commenced his service as an enlisted nuclear Submarine Sonar Technician in 1961, was selected for the Navy Enlisted Scientific Education Program in 1966, and graduated from University of Washington in Marine Physics and Meteorology in 1969. He returned to nuclear submarines as the Navy's first Poseidon Weapons Officer. Subsequently, he served as Navigator and Diving Officer on both catamaran mother vessels for the Deep Submergence Rescue Vehicle. Then he joined the Submarine Development Group One out of San Diego as the Officer-in-Charge of the Test Operations Group, conducting "deep-ocean surveillance and data acquisition"—which forms the basis for his Cold War novel *Operation Ivy Bells*.

In NOAA Dr. Williscroft directed diving operations throughout the Pacific and Atlantic. As a certified diving instructor for both the National Association of Underwater Instructors (NAUI) and the Multinational Diving Educators Association (MDEA), he taught over 3,000 individuals both basic and advanced SCUBA diving. He authored four diving books, developed the first NAUI drysuit course, developed advanced curricula for mixed gas and other specialized diving modes, and developed and taught a NAUI course on the Math and Physics of Advanced Diving. His doctoral dissertation for California Coast University, *A System for Protecting SCUBA Divers from the Hazards of Contaminated Water* was published by the U.S.

Department of Commerce and distributed to Port Captains worldwide. He also served three shipboard years in the high Arctic conducting scientific baseline studies, and thirteen months at the geographic South Pole in charge of National Science Foundation atmospheric projects.

Dr. Williscroft has written extensively on terrorism and related subjects. He is the author of a popular book on current events published by Pelican Publishing: *The Chicken Little Agenda—Debunking Experts' Lies*, now in its second edition as an eBook, and a new children's book series, *Starman Jones*, in collaboration with Dr. Frank Drake, world-famous director of the Carl Sagan Center for the Study of Life in the Universe and the SETI Institute.

Dr. Williscroft's 1st novel in *The Starchild Trilogy*, *Slingshot*, tells the story of the construction of the world's first Space Launch Loop. *Slingshot* was launched at the Seattle International Space Elevator Conference in August 2015. His 2nd novel in *The Starchild Trilogy*, *The Starchild Compact*, is based on the discovery that Saturn's moon Iapetus is actually a derelict starship, and how Earth explorers eventually meet with the "Founders," who originally arrived on the starship and populated the Earth long ago. The 3rd book in *The Starchild Trilogy*, *The Iapetus Federation*, the Federation expands Solar Systemwide, while a new Caliphate sweeps Earth. The Starchild Institute creates wormhole portals to enable the Exodus. Earth becomes medieval, while human focus shifts to the Iapetus Federation. Humans settle every potentially habitable spot in the Solar System and begin expanding into the rest of the Galaxy.

*The SWIC Daedalus Files* takes place in the world of *Slingshot*. In four short stories, *Daedalus*, *Daedalus LEO*, *Daedalus Squad*, and *Daedalus Combat*, Dr. Williscroft follows the U.S. Navy SEALS Winged Insertion Command (SWIC) and its development of the *Gryphon* hard wingsuit for combat drops from Low Earth Orbit

Dr. Williscroft is an active member of the venerable Adventurers' Club of Los Angeles, where he is the former Editor of the Club's monthly magazine. He is a board member of the Colorado Authors' League. He lives in Centennial, Colorado, with his wife, Jill, whom he met upon his return from the South Pole in 1982 and finally married in 2011, and their twin college boys (when they are home from school).

# OTHER WORKS BY ROBERT G. WILLISCROFT

Please visit Amazon.com to discover other eBooks by Robert Williscroft and your favorite online or Brick & Mortar bookseller for their paper versions:

## Current events:

*The Chicken Little Agenda—Debunking "Experts'" Lies*

## Children's books:

*The Starman Jones Series:*
    *Starman Jones: A Relativity Birthday Present*
    *Starman Jones Goes to the Dogs (scheduled for release in 2019)*

## Short Stories:

*The SWIC Daedalus Files:*
    *Daedalus*
    *Daedalus—LEO*
    *Daedalus—Squad (scheduled for release in 2019)*
    *Daedalus—Combat (scheduled for release in 2019)*

## Novels:

*Mac McDowell Missions*
    *Operation Ivy Bells*
    *Operation Snow Cone (Scheduled for release 2020)*

*The Starchild Trilogy:*
>   *Slingshot*
>   *The Starchild Compact*
>   *The Iapetus Federation*

*The Oort Chronicles:*
>   *Icicle—A Tensor Matrix (scheduled for release in 2019)*
>   *The Oort—Interstellar Consequences (scheduled for release in 2020)*
>   *Oort Andromeda—Galactic Diaspora (scheduled for release in 2020)*

# CONNECT WITH
# ROBERT G. WILLISCROFT

I really appreciate you reading my book! Here are my social media coordinates:

Friend me on Facebook: *https://www.facebook.com/robert.williscroft*

Follow me on Twitter: *@RGWilliscroft*

Like my Amazon author page:
*http://www.amazon.com/Robert-G.-Williscroft/e/B001JP52AS*

Subscribe to my blog: Thrawn Rickle

Connect on LinkedIn: *http://www.linkedin.com/in/argee/*

Visit my website: *http://robertwilliscroft.com*

# DAEDALUS LEO
# GLOSSARY

**Atoll**—A ring-shaped reef, island, or chain of islands formed of coral.

**Baker Compound**—The *Slingshot* facility on Baker Island.

**CPA**—Closest point of approach.

**EMT**—Emergency Medical Technician.

**Gryphon-7**—A wingsuit-like carapace strapped on the body. It stopped short of the feet, but in flight could extend to a full two meters, stretching beyond the feet. It attached to the legs and arms, with special controls for each hand, and had a broad Velcro band across the midriff. It had extensible delta wings with a three-meter wingspan. The back end contained a small steerable hypergolic rocket engine, and the left and right wings each contained pressurized hypergolic fuel components. Switches in the hand units controlled the fuel valves. The *Gryphon* had a heads-up display with height-over-ground, airspeed, groundspeed, compass, and GPS coordinates superimposed on a map, plus various system readouts.

**Gryphon-10**—Like *Gryphon-7* with some radical changes including full body armor with circulating fuel for heat protection, an increased surface area using dimples, wrinkles, and rolls that dramatically boosted heat shedding, and it incorporated a new type of polymer that was stronger, lighter, and more heat resistant than anything before. The biggest change was Mother, the guidance computer unit designed to act on its calculations before the human pilot was even aware of them.

Still man-transportable, although more ungainly than *Gryphon-7*. Its unpowered glide ratio was 14-1, and it could fly 100 level klicks under power.

**Howland Island**—A coral island in the equatorial Pacific about sixty-five kilometers north of Baker Island. It was the destination of Amelia Earhart when she disappeared.

**Hypergolic fuel**– Fuel that ignites spontaneously when the individual fuel elements come into contact.

**Hypergolic rocket**– A rocket that uses hypergolic fuel.

**Keith Lofstrom**—Inventor of the Launch Loop.

**Kick thruster**—A small, reigniteable solid-state rocket attached to a capsule or pallet, used for vector changes after release from the rail, or to slow down a capsule or pallet used to transit from Baker to Jarvis. The rocket was extinguished with an iris-like very strong magnetic field that sliced through the solid fuel column just above the burn.

**Klick**—Slang word for kilometer.

**Launch Loop**— A means for getting into space without using rockets. Consists of a segmented soft iron ribbon moving at orbital speed, starting at ground level, elevating itself to eighty km, following the Earth's curvature for 1,800 km, returning to ground level, and then tracing the path back forming a continuous loop. Two elevator-equipped skytowers extend from the ground to the loop. At the top are two skyports at eighty km altitude. Personnel capsules and cargo pallets are magnetically coupled to the moving loop and launched into space.

**Launch Loop International**—The company that and manages Slingshot.

**Launch pouch**—Attaches to the capsule underside, enabling magnetic acceleration of the capsule by the rail.

**LEO**—Low Earth Orbit

**Mach number**—The ratio of the speed of a body to the speed of sound in the surrounding medium.

**Maglev train**—A magnetically levitated train; it floats above the track propelled by magnetism.

**Rail**—Common term for the portion of the launch loop between the skyports.

**Ribbon**—Common term for the soft-iron tube that is the heart of the launch loop.

**SEAL**—An acronym for *Sea Air and Land*; a member of a Naval Special Warfare unit trained for unconventional warfare.

**Skyport**—The structure at the top of the skytower.

**Skyrail**—An alternative name for a Space Elevator or Launch Loop.

**Skytower**—The elevator-like set of cables that extends from the Skyport to the island below.

**Slingshot**—The Space Launch Loop between Baker and Jarvis Islands in the equatorial Pacific.

**Socket**—The attachment point on the island for the skytower.

**SWIC**—SEALS Winged Insertion Command

**UV light**—Ultraviolet light.

**Wingsuit** –Aa suit with fabric filling the gaps between stretched out arms and ankles, and between the legs, enabling the wearer to glide through the air.

# Fresh Ink Group
## Independent Multi-media Publisher
## Fresh Ink Group / Push Pull Press

❧

Hardcovers
Softcovers
All Ebook Platforms
Audiobooks
Worldwide Distribution

❧

Indie Author Services
Book Development, Editing, Proofing
Graphic/Cover Design
Video/Trailer Production
Website Creation
Social Media Management
Writing Contests
Writers' Blogs
Podcasts

❧

Authors
Editors
Artists
Experts
Professionals

❧

**FreshInkGroup.com**
**info@FreshInkGroup.com**
**Twitter: @FreshInkGroup**
**Facebook.com/FreshInkGroup**
**LinkedIn: Fresh Ink Group**

# Also by Robert G. Williscroft

THE STARCHILD TRILOGY begins with building a Space Launch Loop enabling massive movement off Earth and subsequent settlement of Cislunar-Space, Mars, and beyond. SLINGSHOT is the story of the struggle behind constructing the largest machine ever built stretching between Baker and Jarvis Islands in the Equatorial Pacific, and how the men and women behind Slingshot overcome the project's physical, economic, and human obstacles. In THE STARCHILD COMPACT, a team exploring Saturn's moon Iapetus discovers it to be a derelict starship, and meets the Founders, remnants of an ancient, advanced race, the Ectarians, that arrived in the Solar System 150,000 years ago. Together, they create the Starchild Institute governed by a document they call the Starchild Compact to further develop and introduce Ectarian technology to the Solar System. Using Ectarian technology, they develop near lightspeed spacecraft, artificial wormholes, FTL starships, and human longevity. As human colonies expand into the Solar System, they form a governing coalition: THE IAPETUS FEDERATION. While a united Islam pursues a global Jihad that rages across the planet putting millions to the sword, the Federation enables an exodus from Earth using artificial wormholes. From hand-to-hand combat in the oceans, to battles on Earth's surface, to the challenge of living off-Earth and reaching for the stars, our heroes fight to survive and to expand humankind to the far reaches of the universe.

# More at RobertWilliscroft.com

CPSIA information can be obtained
at www.ICGtesting.com
Printed in the USA
BVHW041713081019
560541BV00003B/4/P

9 781947 867604